This igloo book belongs to:

..................................

igloobooks

Published in 2013
by Igloo Books Ltd
Cottage Farm
Sywell
NN6 0BJ
www.igloobooks.com

SHE001 1113
4 6 8 10 9 7 5 3
ISBN 978-0-85780-856-1

Printed and manufactured in China

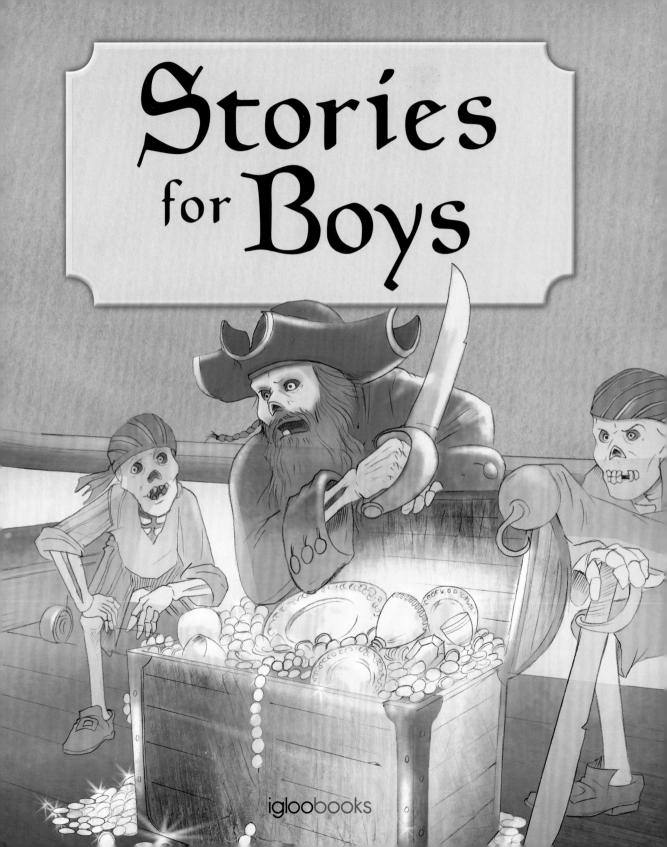

# Stories for Boys

igloobooks

# Contents

# Pinocchio

O nce upon a time, an old carpenter, called Geppetto, lived all by himself. He was so lonely, he decided to make a wooden puppet to keep him company.

In his workshop, Geppetto carved a little wooden head, a wooden body and wooden arms and legs. Then he dressed the puppet in clothes, like a real boy. "I will call him Pinocchio," said Geppetto. The old carpenter looked at the puppet. "I wish you were real," he said. "I have always wanted a son."

Suddenly, by some strange, unseen magic, the wooden puppet began to move. Geppetto stared in amazement as it jumped up from the work bench and began to run around the workshop, shouting and waving its arms.

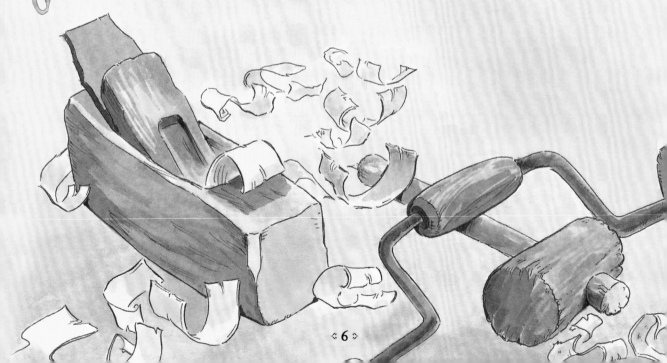

Geppetto was overjoyed. He did not understand why his wooden puppet had come to life, but he was very happy. "Pinocchio," said Geppetto, "I am your father and tomorrow you will go to school. Maybe, one day, if you learn enough, you will become a real boy."

That night, when Pinocchio went to bed, he dreamed that a beautiful fairy visited him. "I am the Blue Fairy who looks after all boys – real, or wooden," she said. "I have brought you a friend to help you to be good." The Blue Fairy waved her wand and a tiny cricket appeared.

The cricket was able to speak. "Hello, Pinocchio," it said. "I will be your friend and help you to behave properly, like a real boy. Tomorrow, we shall go to school together."

The next morning, Pinocchio went downstairs with the cricket. Geppetto was very proud that his little wooden son was going to school. "Here are five gold coins to buy school books with," he said. "It's all the money I have in the world, so spend it wisely."

"Yes, Father," said Pinocchio. But the wooden puppet was lying. He did not want to go to school, or spend the money on school books. Suddenly, Pinocchio's wooden nose grew longer. Geppetto looked at it and frowned. "Pinocchio," he said, "why is your nose growing?" But the puppet just grabbed the gold coins, shoved them into his pocket and ran out of the door.

The clever cricket knew that the puppet's nose had changed because he had told a lie. From that moment on, each time Pinocchio lied, his nose grew longer.

Meanwhile, outside the house, Pinocchio heard lovely music. "Let's go to school," said the cricket, but Pinocchio ignored him and followed the music, which led to a travelling puppet theater.

"I am going to stay here and become a performer," said Pinocchio. "My father won't mind." But when he said this, Pinocchio's nose grew, which meant he was lying.

The cricket tried to stop Pinocchio, but the puppet would not listen. Instead of going to school, he travelled with the theater to a distant land, near the sea.

Poor Geppetto looked everywhere for his precious, wooden son. But Pinocchio was nowhere to be found.

After many days, the cricket persuaded Pinocchio to go back home. They set off and Pinocchio jangled Geppetto's five gold coins in his pockets, as he walked.

Nearby, a cunning cat and a sly fox heard the money jangling. "Where are you going, little wooden boy?" they asked. Pinocchio told them that he was going home to see his father. "Your father will make you go to school, when you could be having fun in the Land of Play," said the sly fox.

"However," said the cat. "Nobody who has any money can get in. Money isn't allowed in the Land of Play."

Pinocchio gave the fox and the cat all of his money. He would not listen to the cricket who told him not to. "Tell me the way to the Land of Play," begged Pinocchio, "I want to go there now."

The cat and the fox told Pinocchio where to go. Then they ran off, laughing at how they had tricked the silly puppet out of his money.

"Please, Pinocchio, go home to your father," pleaded the cricket. "I don't want to see my father," snapped the puppet. Suddenly, his nose grew longer. Pinocchio secretly missed Geppetto, but he refused to go home.

The Land of Play was a huge fair. There were sweets and rides and lots of games to play. It was filled with children who didn't want to go to school and Pinocchio spent many weeks there.

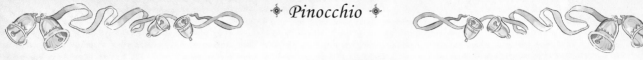

Meanwhile, Geppetto was sick with worry. He searched all over the land for Pinocchio, but there was no sign of him anywhere. Finally, Geppetto reached the sea. "Pinocchio must have crossed the water," he thought. Geppetto built a raft to look for his son. However, far out on the ocean, the raft was swallowed by a huge shark and Geppetto found himself in its belly.

In the Land of Play, Pinocchio didn't notice the days passing until his ears began to feel strange. They were long and floppy, like donkey's ears. Then, when he looked behind him, Pinocchio noticed that he had grown a donkey's tail.

"All children who stay here turn into donkeys," said the cricket. "We must escape, before you become one, too, Pinocchio."

However, the gates of the Land of Play were shut. The only way out was by sea, so Pinocchio and the cricket jumped into the water.

Great waves rolled and the wild sea tossed the pair up and down. After many hours, a huge shark swam by and swallowed the exhausted friends.

It was dark inside the shark's belly. Suddenly, Pinocchio heard a voice – it was Geppetto! "I'm sorry that I lied and ran away, Father," sobbed Pinocchio.

Geppetto hugged his wooden son. "I forgive you," he said. They all danced for joy and the movement gave the shark such a bellyache, it spat them out and they were washed up on the shore.

After that, Pinocchio promised to be good and this time, his nose didn't grow. Instead, the Blue Fairy appeared. "Pinocchio, you have learned to tell the truth," she said. "Now you are a real boy."

Pinocchio felt the donkey ears and tail disappear. Suddenly, his wooden body was soft and warm. He was a real boy! Pinocchio, Geppetto and the cricket returned home and lived in peace and happiness ever after.

# Sinbad and the Giant

O nce upon a time, there was a fearless sailor named Sinbad. Sinbad and his brave crew sailed the seven seas, exploring strange, new lands and always looking for rare and exotic goods to trade. Often, their searches led them into dangerous adventures, but none was as deadly as Sinbad's encounter with the one-eyed giant.

Sinbad was sailing back to his home, with a ship laden with treasure, when a mighty storm blew up. Huge waves rose higher than the mast and crashed down on the deck. Thunder rattled above the ship and lightning blasted down to strike the mast. Sinbad and his men were thrown into the sea. When the storm cleared, the sailors found themselves washed up on a deserted island. There was no sign of their ship.

The crew explored the island, but the only animals they could find were a herd of sheep grazing on a grassy hill. As Sinbad climbed the hill, he saw a mighty fortress on the other side. Its great doors were open, so Sinbad and his men stumbled inside. There, they found an empty courtyard. It was lined with tall doors, all of which were closed. Sinbad and his men were exhausted. They soon fell asleep in the courtyard.

The sailors woke up to a thundering sound so loud, they thought the storm had returned. But it was not the storm. A flock of sheep had run into the courtyard. They were followed by a mighty giant. It was his footsteps that were making so much noise. The giant was as tall as ten men standing on each others' shoulders. He was fierce and foul-smelling and he had a single eye in the middle of his forehead.

The men tried to escape, but the giant had closed the great doors behind them. "What's this?" roared the giant. "I can smell human beings!" The giant peered at them with his huge eye. Sinbad noticed that the giant couldn't see very well. However, the giant managed to grab Sinbad. "You're very skinny," said the giant, throwing Sinbad to the ground. He picked up another man and felt him all over. "Another skinny one," he said, grumpily, throwing the sailor down.

The ship's cook was a much fatter man. He tried to run from the giant, but the giant scooped him up easily. "That's more like it," bellowed the giant. "Tomorrow night, I will make a big fire and roast you for my dinner!" The giant opened one of the big doors and went into his castle, leaving Sinbad and his men trapped in the gloomy courtyard.

The poor cook was terrified that he was going to be eaten. "Don't worry," said Sinbad. "When the giant lets his sheep out tomorrow morning, we'll rush out, too." So, the next morning, when the giant opened his gates to let the sheep out, Sinbad and his men tried to leave. But the giant saw them and slammed the heavy gate shut before they could get out.

That night, when the giant came back in, he made a fire and tried to find the cook. But Sinbad was too clever for the giant. He hid the fat cook in a pile of sheepskins that were lying in a corner of the courtyard. Then he marched up to the giant. "Look what you've done to me," said Sinbad, trying to sound like the cook. "I'm so frightened, I've become nothing more than skin and bone."

The giant picked Sinbad up. "You're not worth eating," he said. He threw Sinbad and his men some mutton, which they ate, hungrily. "I'll fatten you up, then eat you tomorrow night," said the giant, going to bed inside his castle.

"How will we get out?" asked the fat cook, coming out from under the sheepskins. Sinbad looked at the sheepskins. "I think I have a plan," he said.

The next morning, when the giant went to let his sheep out, he found that Sinbad and his crew had built a big, smoky fire. The giant could hardly see anything. "You're not getting out," he yelled. As he let his sheep out, he felt along each one's back, to make sure it wasn't Sinbad, or his men. "That's funny," said the giant. "I have more sheep than I thought."

The giant didn't realise that Sinbad and his crew had put sheepskins over their backs and walked out on all fours, pretending to be sheep.

Sinbad and his men ran to the other side of the island and chopped down some trees to make big rafts. By evening, they were almost ready to sail.

However, when the giant herded his sheep back to his castle that night, he realised that the men were gone. "I've been tricked!" he boomed and Sinbad could hear it from the other side of the island.

The giant stomped all over the island, looking all around with his one, giant eye. As Sinbad tied the last of the logs to the raft, he made sure everyone was on board. "Set sail!" he cried and the men raised the sheepskin sails.

Just as they were pushing off the raft, the giant saw them. He waded right into the sea. The sailors paddled as fast as they could, but the wind kept blowing them backwards. The giant raised his huge hands and tried to smash the raft.

"Cut down the mast," cried Sinbad. The sailors were amazed, but they did what they were told. The tall mast of the raft toppled over and struck the angry giant on the head. The giant sank right to the bottom of the ocean and never troubled anybody again.

"Now we are stuck in the sea without a mast," said the fat cook, sadly. "We'll never get home."
"There's something on the horizon," said one of the men. "It's our ship!"

Sure enough, Sinbad's ship had survived the storm. Sinbad and his men sailed back home with all their treasure and a wonderful story of a one-eyed giant to tell.

# Jack and the Beanstalk

Once upon a time, a poor widow lived with her only son, Jack. He was an adventurous boy who was always getting into mischief, but he loved his mother dearly. Jack and his mother never had any money and their only possession was a black and white cow.

One day, there was no food left in the house and the cow wouldn't give any milk. "We shall have to sell the cow," said Jack's mother, sadly. "Take her to market tomorrow and get the best price you can for her."

The next day, Jack led the cow to the market. On the way, he met a strange-looking man. "That's a fine cow you have there," said the man. "Will you sell her to me for these beans? They are magic beans, as you will see."

"My mother will be cross," Jack thought to himself. But the magic beans sounded very exciting. So, he exchanged the cow for the beans and went home.

When Jack's mother heard what he had done, she was furious. "You sold our only possession for a handful of beans. Now we have nothing!" She threw the beans out of the window and sent Jack to bed.

The next morning, Jack woke up and looked out of his window. In the tiny garden, an enormous beanstalk had sprouted from the beans. It went so high up into the sky, its top disappeared into the clouds.

"They really were magic beans," said Jack, in amazement. "I wonder what's at the top of the beanstalk?"

Jack began to climb the beanstalk. He climbed and climbed until he was so high, he could see the countryside for miles around and his cottage looked no bigger than a dot.

Jack climbed even higher until he was above the clouds. He finally reached the top of the beanstalk and was surprised to find that he was in a magical land. Everything was enormous. The daisies towered above him. The grass was like a forest. He even saw a beetle as big as a cat.

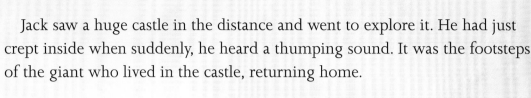

Jack saw a huge castle in the distance and went to explore it. He had just crept inside when suddenly, he heard a thumping sound. It was the footsteps of the giant who lived in the castle, returning home.

Jack sneaked inside a huge oven and watched. The giant was carrying three big bags of gold. Suddenly, he sniffed the air and bellowed,

"Fee, fi, fo, fum,
I smell the blood of an Englishman.
Be he alive, or be he dead,
I'll grind his bones to make my bread!"

The giant searched everywhere for Jack, but he didn't look in the oven. Eventually, the giant sat at his kitchen table and fell asleep. Jack opened the oven door and crept out. He grabbed one of the bags of money and sneaked back to the beanstalk, then climbed down carefully. His mother was delighted to see him and they had enough money to live on for many months.

However, eventually, the money ran out. "I must climb the beanstalk to the castle again," said Jack and he climbed to the top of the beanstalk once more. The giant was out again but, on his enormous kitchen table was a beautiful hen. Jack was about to snatch it, when he heard the giant return. The giant cried,

"Fee, fi, fo, fum,
I smell the blood of an Englishman.
Be he alive, or be he dead,
I'll grind his bones to make my bread!"

Jack hid in a giant mouse hole, so the giant could not find him. The giant sat at the table and pulled out a little golden harp and started to play it. Suddenly, the hen laid an egg of pure gold. The giant leaned back on his chair in satisfaction and was soon fast asleep.

Jack came out of his hiding place, put the hen under his arm and crept out of the kitchen. Suddenly, the hen let out a loud squawk. The giant woke up with a start and saw that his hen was gone, but Jack was already charging back to the beanstalk.

At home, Jack tried to get the hen to lay a golden egg, but it just clucked, sadly. "We need the golden harp," said Jack. So he climbed the beanstalk one more time, until he was back in the land above the clouds. Searching through the giant's house, Jack found the harp in an enormous cupboard. Just as he was about to creep away with it, he heard the giant bellowing,

"Fee, fi, fo, fum,
I smell the blood of an Englishman.
Be he alive, or be he dead,
I'll grind his bones to make my bread!"

Jack grabbed the harp and ran out of the castle with it. However, the harp was magical and could speak. "I'm being stolen!" it cried out.

The giant thundered after Jack who ran as fast as he could, for fear that he would be caught and his bones ground up to make the giant's bread.

At last, Jack reached the beanstalk and climbed down. Behind him, the giant jumped onto the beanstalk and began climbing down, too.

At the bottom of the beanstalk, Jack fetched an axe. He chopped and chopped at the beanstalk with all his might until the beanstalk wobbled and tottered and crashed down. The giant fell to the ground and was so shocked, he ran away and never came back.

Jack and his mother played the magic harp to the hen and it began to lay golden eggs. With so much gold, Jack and his mother were never poor again and they lived happily ever after.

# The Boy Who Cried Wolf

Once upon a time, there lived a young shepherd boy. Every day, he took his sheep up the side of a mountain and let them graze. Every night, he took the sheep back down to their pen in the farm. All day long, the shepherd boy watched the sheep. It was very dull. "I wish I had some other people up here with me," he thought. "But nobody wants to walk all the way up the mountain, just to see me."

So, the shepherd boy ran down the mountain to where his older brother was farming the land, with several big farm workers helping him. "Help, a wolf is attacking my sheep!" cried the shepherd boy, jumping around and waving his hands.

At once, his brother and the farm workers rushed all the way up the mountain, puffing and panting. "Where's the wolf?" they cried. "There's no wolf," admitted the shepherd boy. "It was just a joke."

His brother and the farmhands went back down the mountain in a very bad mood. The shepherd boy just giggled. "That was fun," he thought.

The next day, the shepherd boy decided to try his trick again. This time, he ran all the way down into the small village by the farm.

"Help, a wolf is attacking my sheep!" he cried. "Come, quickly." All the people in the village followed the shepherd boy up the mountain.

"Ha, ha, there's no wolf," said the shepherd boy, when the people from the village reached the sheep. "It was just a trick." The shepherd boy rolled around on the grass, laughing, while the villagers left, angrily.

The next day, the shepherd boy decided to try his trick on an old shepherd who lived on the other side of the mountain. He ran round to the shepherd and cried, "Help, a wolf is attacking my sheep!"

The old shepherd looked hard at him until the shepherd boy had to look away. "You're lying," said the old shepherd. "Now leave, before I set my sheepdog on you!"

The shepherd boy ran away, annoyed that his trick hadn't worked.

The next day, the shepherd boy saw a big, grey shape slinking behind his sheep. It was a wolf.

Quick as a flash, the shepherd boy ran down the mountain to the farm. "Wolf! Wolf!" he yelled. "There's a wolf on the mountain."
His brother and his brother's friends laughed at him. "We're not going to fall for that one again," his brother said.

So, the shepherd boy dashed into the village. "Please, help me!" he cried. "A real wolf is attacking the sheep."
"Go away," said the people of the village, "we don't have time to listen to your lies."

In despair, the shepherd boy ran back up the mountain. He saw that the wolf was sneaking closer and closer to the sheep.

The shepherd boy ran round the mountain to where the old shepherd sat with his sheepdog. "I know you won't believe me!" cried the shepherd boy. "But a real wolf is about to attack my sheep!"

The old shepherd stared hard at the boy and the boy thought he was going to send him away again. "Come on, then, boy," said the old shepherd, grimly. "There's not a moment to lose." They ran back round the mountain with the old shepherd's sheepdog.

When the sheepdog saw the wolf, it ran at it, growling. The wolf jumped back in surprise and then ran off, its tail between its legs.

After thanking the old shepherd, the shepherd boy went down into the village. He told everyone what had happened. "I'm sorry I lied to you all," said the shepherd boy, sadly. "I don't blame you for not believing me when I said a wolf was attacking my sheep. I'll never lie again."

Soon after, the old shepherd called the shepherd boy around to his side of the mountain. In the old shepherd's hut, the sheepdog had had six tiny puppies. "Take one," said the old shepherd. "It'll help you guard the sheep."

The shepherd boy chose a black and white puppy. It grew up to be a loyal sheepdog and together, the shepherd boy and his dog guarded the sheep well.

After that, the shepherd boy was never lonely. He didn't tell any more lies and he never cried, 'Wolf,' again.

# The Brave Little Donkey

O nce, there was a little donkey who lived with his mother in a field. The little donkey was very happy. All day long he would play and eat juicy, green grass.

However, the little donkey soon grew bigger and the time came for him to be sold so that he could go and work somewhere else.

"You must work hard," said the little donkey's mother. "Just remember that you will always have the three donkey gifts – your bite, your kick and your loud bray."

The donkey was sold to a farmer who lived in a farmhouse with his large family. The donkey loved his new life. He slept in a warm stable, next to the house. The children of the family loved riding the donkey around the farmyard and he was so much a part of the family, he was even allowed inside the farmhouse. Sometimes, late at night, the children would poke a bunch of carrots through the stable door for him to eat.

A band of robbers moved to the area, looking for things to steal. When they saw the farmhouse, they decided to creep in and steal everything they could find.

The easiest way into the farmhouse was through the stables. That night, one of the robbers made a hole in the stable door and reached his hand through to unlock it.

The donkey was sleeping in the stables when he saw the robber's hand poking through the door in the dark. The donkey thought it was a bunch of carrots. He reached over to the hand and bit down hard. The robber ran off in pain and fright.

"The farmer must have a ferocious guard dog," said the robber to his friends. "Look at this bite on my hand. We will have to find a different way in."

The next night, the robbers tried to rob the farmhouse again. The donkey heard a noise and looked out of the stable. He saw the robbers trying to break open the front door of the farmhouse.

The donkey began to bray. It was a very loud sound and made the robbers run away immediately. However, by the time the farmer and his family had come downstairs and out to the stables, the robbers were long gone.

"Why do you make so much noise, donkey?" said the farmer. "You've woken us all up." The farmer was very angry with the donkey, but the donkey knew he had saved the family.

The next day, the donkey was allowed into the kitchen while a great feast was being prepared for a party that night. The donkey was very hungry, because the children had forgotten to feed him that day. When everyone was out, he decided to taste one of the cakes that had been left on the table.

The donkey ate another cake and then another one after that. He even ate the vegetables, the roast beef, the bread and the cheese.

By the time the family came back, all the food was gone and the donkey was standing in the middle of a messy, empty kitchen.

The farmer was furious. "Get out," he said to the donkey. "There'll be no cosy stable for you tonight. As punishment, you'll sleep in the barn."

The donkey was very sorry for what he had done. The barn that night was very cold. It was stacked with big logs and there was hardly enough room to lie down.

The donkey shivered and stuck his head through the window of the barn. He saw the gang of robbers again. They were sneaking into the house through a different door. The donkey tried braying, but the farmer just shouted at him to be quiet.

"I've used my bite and my bray," thought the donkey. "Now it's time for my kick!" Quick as a flash, the donkey kicked the wide, barn doors open. Before the robbers could move, he stood behind the enormous pile of logs and gave them a big kick with his hind legs. The logs rolled out of the barn, onto the robbers, trapping them.

The farmer came downstairs and saw that the brave donkey had trapped the robbers. "Thank you," he said. "You've saved us."

As a reward, the farmer bought the donkey all the carrots he could eat. The children piled his stable with warm hay and the donkey never had to sleep in the cold barn again.

# Ali Baba and the Forty Thieves

**M**any years ago, there were two brothers called Ali Baba and Kassim, who lived in a great, city in the East. Ali Baba was hard-working and honest, but his brother, Kassim, was cruel and greedy. Kassim took all the money that the brothers earned and Ali Baba hardly ever had enough to buy food.

One day, when Ali Baba was out gathering wood in the forest, he heard the sound of many voices. Peering through the trees, he saw a crowd of forty evil-looking thieves carrying large sacks. The leader of the thieves called out, "Quick, we must take this stolen gold into our magic cave."

The thieves were standing by a rocky wall and Ali Baba couldn't see any opening in it. "Open, Sesame," cried the leader. Suddenly, the rocks parted to show an entrance into a cave, filled with treasure. The thieves put the gold in the cave and then the leader cried, "Close, Sesame." The hole in the rock disappeared and the thieves ran away, laughing.

When the thieves had gone, Ali Baba stood in front of the rock. "Open, Sesame!" he shouted. Sure enough, the rock opened to reveal the magic cave.

Inside, the cave was full of gold, jewels and all kinds of treasure. Ali Baba put some of the coins in his pocket. When he turned to go, he found he was trapped inside. The rock had closed behind him. "Open, Sesame," he yelled and the rock opened again.

Ali Baba rushed out of the cave. "Close, Sesame!" he cried and the huge rock sealed the entrance.

When Ali Baba got home, his brother, Kassim, asked him where he had got the coins. Reluctantly, Ali Baba told him about the thieves, the cave and the magic word.

Greedy Kassim wanted all the treasure for himself. That night, he travelled to the cave and called out, "Open, Sesame." The cave opened and Kassim rushed in and stuffed his pockets with treasure. Then he realised that he was shut in. "I'll just say the magic word," thought Kassim. But he had forgotten it. "Open, semolina," he said. "Open, sugary." But, try as he might, Kassim couldn't make the rock move. He was trapped in the cave all night.

The next morning, the forty thieves opened the cave and found Kassim. "Stealing our treasure, are you?" said the leader. "Tie him up and leave him here," he said to his men.

The next day, Ali Baba was worried that Kassim had not returned. He went to the cave and used the magic word to open it. Kassim was lying inside, tied up and helpless. Ali Baba untied his brother and they fled, just as the thieves were returning to the cave. The thieves chased them all the way to the city. Ali Baba and Kassim escaped from the thieves in the crowded marketplace. Later on, however, the leader saw the brothers going into their house.

"Tonight, when they are asleep, we will come and capture them," said the leader of the thieves. He marked the door with chalk, so the thieves would find it that night.

Luckily, Kassim's clever servant girl, Morgiana, had seen the leader mark the door. She went to Ali Baba and told him. "I have a plan," said Morgiana. She went around all the local houses and marked the doors with chalk. That night, the forty thieves looked for the house, but it was impossible to find the right one.

The cunning thieves kept watch that day and the leader spotted Ali Baba leaving his house. This time, the leader made a chip in the front doorstep. However, he hadn't counted on clever Morgiana. She saw him make the chip and went around all the local houses, chipping their doorsteps, too. That night, the forty thieves couldn't find the house again.

After that, the leader was more determined than ever to catch Ali Baba and Kassim. Soon, he worked out a cunning plan. With some of his stolen gold, he bought forty big, clay jars. The thieves climbed in the jars and the leader put them on a cart and took them to the marketplace. The leader disguised himself as a merchant and waited.

Soon, Ali Baba walked through the marketplace. "Kind sir," called the leader. "I have forty jars of olive oil that need to be stored. If you will put them in your house for one night, I will give you a gold coin."

"Of course," said Ali Baba. The leader took the jars into Ali Baba's house and when Ali Baba was gone, he climbed into the last empty one. The thieves planned to jump out of the jars and capture Ali Baba and Kassim that same night.

Once again, Morgiana was too clever for them. "The thieves are in the jars," she told Ali Baba. So, Ali Baba, Kassim and Morgiana tied up the lids of the jars, so they couldn't be opened. Then they carefully loaded the jars onto a cart and drove out of the city.

The thieves knew that they were moving. They shouted and struggled to get out of the jars, but they were trapped inside. Ali Baba drove the cart to the top of a big hill. Ali Baba, Kassim and Morgiana pushed the jars down the steep slope.

The jars rolled and rolled, all the way down the hillside and cracked at the bottom. The thieves were so frightened that they ran off and were never seen again.

Now, Ali Baba and Kassim were free to take all the treasure they wanted from the magic cave. In admiration at Morgiana's cleverness, Ali Baba married her and they lived happily ever after.

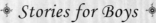

# Aladdin

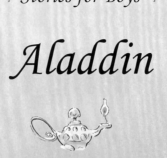

Long ago, in a great city, there lived a poor, hungry orphan boy named Aladdin. He had no home of his own, so he had to live on the streets and steal food to survive.

One day, a wealthy-looking man called out to Aladdin in the marketplace. Aladdin thought the man was about to punish him for stealing and he tried to hide. "Don't be afraid," said the man. "I am your long-lost uncle, Abenazer. If you will help me, Aladdin, together we will make our fortune."

Aladdin didn't know that Abenazer was not really his uncle, but a wicked magician. Abenazer wanted a magic lamp that lay in an enchanted cave nearby, but he was cowardly and wanted Aladdin to get it for him.

Abenazer took Aladdin to the cave entrance, which was a small hole that led down steep stairs. "You may take all the treasure you find inside," said Abenazer. "Just bring me the dirty old lamp from the middle of the cave."

Aladdin went into the cave. He had never seen so much treasure. Gold was piled in heaps on the floor and the walls of the cave were covered with precious stones. Aladdin filled his pockets with jewels. He found a gold ring on the floor and put it on his finger.

Aladdin found the old lamp on a large stone in the middle of the cave. He took the lamp, but the moment it was in his hands, the floor started to shake. Aladdin looked up to find the entrance to the cave closing above him. Climbing as fast as he could, he reached the opening of the cave. "Help me out, Uncle," cried Aladdin.

"Give me the lamp first," said Abenazer. He tried to grab the lamp, but he knocked Aladdin, who was still holding it, down the rocky staircase. Aladdin tumbled back down into the cave and when he looked up, the entrance had closed behind him.

Aladdin sat in the dark, wondering what to do. He was trapped in the cave. "That man was no uncle of mine," he said, rubbing the dirty lamp to clean it. "How I wish I had some light in here."

Suddenly, a mighty, green genie whooshed from the spout of the lamp. The genie made more lamps appear, so the cave was flooded with light.

"I am the genie of the lamp. My wish is your command. What is your next wish, Master?" said the genie.

Aladdin was amazed. "I wish I were at home," he said. The genie clicked his fingers and Aladdin was back in the marketplace, surrounded by the jewels he was carrying.

From then on, the genie appeared every time Aladdin rubbed the lamp. It could make all of Aladdin's wishes come true. "I wish for a great palace!" cried Aladdin. The ground shook and a mighty, marble palace rose from the desert. It was bigger than the palace of the sultan himself.

Soon, Aladdin was the richest man in the city. He married the sultan's daughter and they lived happily in their desert palace.

However, Abenazer had not forgotten Aladdin. When he found out that Aladdin had the lamp, he came up with a plan to get the lamp and use its power for himself.

Abenazer disguised himself as a poor lamp-seller. Then, he went to Aladdin's palace with a cart full of new lamps, "New lamps for old!" he cried.

Aladdin's wife didn't know that Aladdin's lamp was magical. She gave Abenazer the old magic lamp, in return for a shiny new one.

As soon as Abenazer had the lamp, he told the genie to take away all Aladdin's wealth and his palace. Abenazer made himself sultan and imprisoned Aladdin's wife. Aladdin was a poor man, once again.

All that Aladdin had left was the gold ring he had taken from the enchanted cave. "I must sell it to buy food," Aladdin thought. "But I don't know how I can get my wife and my palace back."

Aladdin cleaned the ring with an old rag and suddenly, a great, blue genie whooshed out of it. "I am the genie of the ring," said the genie. "What is your wish?"

Aladdin asked the genie of the ring to restore his power, but the genie could not. "The genie of the lamp is more powerful than me," explained the genie of the ring. "I cannot reverse his magic."

Aladdin asked the genie to take him to Abenazer. In the blink of an eye, he was outside the sultan's palace. Through the windows, he could see that Abenazer had become Sultan.

Aladdin thought of a cunning plan to get his lamp back. "Genie of the ring," he said. "I wish for a potion that will send anyone who drinks it to sleep."
"Your wish is my command, Master," said the genie. It conjured up a bottle of the potion.

Aladdin sneaked into the palace, past Abenazer's guards and found his wife. He gave her the bottle of potion and told her his plan.

Aladdin went to hide and his wife called to Abenazer, "Let me out of this prison and I'll marry you."

Abenazer let Aladdin's wife out and she dropped the potion into his drink. Abenazer started to yawn and soon he was asleep, with the lamp under his arm.

When Aladdin was sure that Abenazer was asleep, he came out of his hiding place. He pulled the lamp from Abenazer's grasp and quickly rubbed it before Abenazer could awake. "Restore my palace and banish Abenazer forever!" cried Aladdin to the genie of the lamp.

In the blink of an eye, Aladdin and his wife were back in their own, splendid palace. The genie sent Abenazer, far, far away, to the other side of the world and Aladdin and his wife lived happily every after.

# The Pig That Flew

Once upon a time, a poor farmer and his wife lived on a tiny farm by a brook. The farmer tended his sheep, while the farmer's wife grew vegetables in their little garden. Life was hard for the farmer and his wife and they rarely had enough food to eat.

One day, when the farmer's wife was selling vegetables at the market, she saw a man selling a piglet. The piglet had small, stumpy wings made of white feathers, like a goose's. "All the other pigs have been sold, but nobody wants one with wings," said the man. The piglet looked very small and sad.

The farmer's wife took pity on the piglet. "I'll buy it," she said. "When it grows up, perhaps we can fatten it up and eat it?"

So, the man tied some string around the pig's neck and gave it to the farmer's wife. "You never know," he said, "this pig may make your fortune, one day."

To the farmer's wife's surprise, the piglet fluttered up into the air. She had took to hold on tight to the string to stop it flying away. The farmer's wife carried the piglet home, like a balloon on a string.

The farmer wasn't very pleased when he saw what his wife had spent their last pennies on. The farmer's wife took the piglet off its string inside the farmhouse.

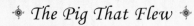

It zoomed around, knocking over ornaments and leaving hoof prints on the ceiling. "Don't worry," said the farmer's wife. "When it grows up, maybe we can fatten it up and eat it."

It wasn't long before the flying pig grew so large, it was too big to keep in the house. The farmer took it outside and let it go. "I'm sorry," said the farmer to the pig, "But we can't afford to feed you any more." The pig took off and flew away over the hills.

The next morning, the farmer and his wife were woken up by grunting noise, outside their window. The flying pig had returned. He had a bronze chain in his mouth. "I suppose he can come back, if he behaves himself," said the farmer.

The farmer sold the chain and had enough money to buy food for a while. The farmer even built the pig a sty.

Soon enough, the money ran out, so the farmer's wife went to dig up vegetables to sell at the market. But all the vegetables were gone. The pig had eaten every last one.

The farmer angrily took the pig to the top of a high hill and chased it off. The pig fluttered its wings and flew away, sadly.

But the next morning, the pig was back and this time it had a silver necklace in its mouth.

The farmer let the pig stay in the sty again. "But if he does anything else, he's gone for good," said the farmer. He sold the necklace and again they had enough food for a while.

Only a few days later, the farmer went to get the sheep from the fields. He found the pig flying through the air, chasing the sheep in all directions. It took the farmer hours to round them up. When he got back to the farm, the farmer was so angry, he chased the pig around and around the sty. The pig flew away over the hills in fright.

The next morning, the pig was back again, with a gold crown in its mouth. "Where does it go?" the farmer's wife wondered.
"I don't care," said the farmer. "Tomorrow, we'll take it to the market and sell it. Someone else can fatten it up and eat it. Then we'll be rid of it for good."

That afternoon, a gigantic storm raged over the farm. The farmer rushed inside. "I must get the sheep to higher ground," he said to his wife. "The river is flooding and they will all be drowned."

The farmer tried to reach the sheep, but soon the water was so deep that he couldn't move out of the house. Water began to pour in through the doors and windows.

"We must climb on the roof, or we'll drown!" said the farmer's wife. When they got up to the roof, they saw an amazing sight. The flying pig had flown over the flood. He was swooping over the sheep, guiding them to the hill where they would be safe.

The waters rose and rose, until they were lapping at the roof. "We're doomed," said the farmer. But the pig flew onto the roof and landed next to them.

The farmer and his wife climbed on the pig's back and the pig flew off, just as the waters covered the top of the roof.

The pig flew a great distance until he landed by a mountain cave. Inside, there was a pile of treasure. "This must be where the pig was getting his presents from," said the farmer. "We're rich!"

The farmer and his wife never had to work again. They lived happily ever after and so did the pig that flew.